To my double agents:
Caroline Walsh and Rebecca Watson – K.G.
To Lucy Napper – N.S.

DAISY: 006 AND A BIT
A RED FOX BOOK 978 1 782 95650 1

First published in Great Britain by The Bodley Head, an imprint of Random House Children's Publishers UK
A Penguin Random House Company

Penguin Random House UK

The Bodley Head edition published 2006
Red Fox edition published 2007
This edition published 2016

1 3 5 7 9 10 8 6 4 2

Text copyright © Kes Gray, 2006
Illustrations copyright © Nick Sharratt, 2006

Penguin Random House is committed to a sustainable future for our business, our readers and our planet.
This book is made from Forest Stewardship Council® certified paper.

MIX
Paper from responsible sources
FSC® C018179

Red Fox Books are published by Random House Children's Publishers UK,
61–63 Uxbridge Road, London W5 5SA

www.randomhousechildrens.co.uk   www.randomhouse.co.uk

Addresses for companies within The Random House Group Limited can be found at: www.randomhouse.co.uk/offices.htm

THE RANDOM HOUSE GROUP Limited Reg. No. 954009

A CIP catalogue record for this book is available from the British Library.

Printed in China

DAISY
006 and a Bit

Kes Gray & Nick Sharratt

RED FOX

Daisy had made up her mind. She wasn't going to be a girl
any more. She was going to be a spy.
She had drawn a spy's moustache on her top lip
with a black felt-tip pen.

She had found some dark glasses in a drawer.

She had found some secret spy gadgets in her mum's
bedroom. All she had to do now was speak in code.

(Code is a special spy language that only spies understand.
Daisy had seen it used in spy films; now this time it was for real.)

Daisy frowned mysteriously and crept unseen into the kitchen.

"Hello, Daisy," said Mum. "What do you want for tea tonight?"

"The ostriches will be swimming in tomato sauce this evening," said Daisy.

(Which, as any spy knows, means "a big portion of chicken nuggets and lots of ketchup, please!")

Daisy's *mum* stared at Daisy and scratched her head.

"Why are you speaking in silly words?" asked Daisy's *mum*.

"They're not silly words," whispered Daisy mysteriously.

"It's secret spy language. And *my* name isn't Daisy any more.
It's 006 and a Bit."

"And what are you intending to do with *my* hairbrush,
006 and a Bit?" asked Daisy's *mum*.

"It's not a hairbrush. It's *my* secret spy telephone,"
said Daisy.

"And where are you going with
my perfume bottle?"
asked Daisy's mum.

"It's not your perfume bottle,"
said Daisy.
"It's my invisible ink."

"And would I be wrong in thinking that is *my* hairdryer?" said Daisy's *mum.*

"Yes," whispered Daisy. "It's not a hairdryer.

It's my secret baddie zapper."

Daisy's *mum* shook her head and went to find the ironing board.

006 and a Bit slipped invisibly into the back garden.

"Hello, Daisy," said her neighbour, "how are you today?"

"Good afternoon, Agent Goldfish," said Daisy.

"Are your fins green or purple today?"

(Which, as any spy knows, means

"I'm fine thanks, Mrs Pike,

how are you?")

Mrs Pike stared strangely at Daisy and
went to mow her grass.

Daisy slipped invisibly across the garden and went to give an important message to Mrs Pike's cat.

"Meet me by the Golden Palace," she whispered, "and bring your furry overcoat."

(which, as any spy knows, means, "Hello, Tiptoes, why don't you come and sit by the shed? I want to stroke you.")

Tiptoes took one look at Daisy's hairdryer
and skedaddled over the wall.

Daisy dabbed on some more invisible ink and peeped
out of the garden gate. "No one will be able
to see me now," she smiled.

"Hello, Daisy," said her best friend Gabby.

"Can you come out to play?"

"The laundry basket is full and the big busy beaver
has many clothes to fold," Daisy said.

(Which, as any spy knows, means, "Hi Gabby! I'll just
ask my mum. She's doing the ironing.")

But Gabby gave Daisy a very strange look and
went to find someone else to play with.

Daisy took off her glasses and walked miserably back indoors.

"What's the matter, 006 and a Bit?" asked her mum.

"Aren't you playing spies any more?"

"No I'm not," sighed Daisy. "No one understands my

spy language. They just look at me as though I'm silly."

Daisy's mum stopped ironing
and put her arm around
Daisy's shoulders.
"That must be because
they're not real spies,"
whispered her mum.
"If they were, they would
understand everything
you are saying."

Daisy trudged into the living room and slumped onto the sofa. "Well they don't understand what I'm saying. There aren't any real spies around here, no one understands me and I'm not being a spy any more. Being a spy is stupid," she grumbled.

Daisy was just about to turn on the TV,
when a mysterious-looking stranger with
a purple moustache and beard poked his
head around the door. He had dark
glasses on, just like Daisy.

"Pssst," whispered the stranger in a
deep mysterious voice. "Have you seen
006 and a Bit anywhere?"

Daisy stared back at the stranger in surprise.
She put her dark glasses on again quickly
and sat up straight.

"Yes I have seen 006 and a Bit!" she nodded.

"That's me! I am 006 and a Bit!"

"That is good news," whispered the stranger,
"because my name is 0021 and a Bit.
I am a real spy too!"

"The coloured sprinkles will be meeting with the chocolate flake on the vanilla ice-cream at tea time," whispered 0021 and a Bit.

"And the crunchy cream biscuits and lemonade will be meeting under the big yellow duvet when the clock strikes twelve," continued the mysterious stranger.

006 and a Bit frowned for a moment and clapped her hands excitedly. "Ooh goody! I know what that means!

We're having my favourite pudding for tea and then a midnight feast in your bed tonight! I'll bring my comic and my torch too!"

Which, as anybody knows, means "Thanks, Mum. You're the best spy in the world!"

DAISY

LITTLE TROUBLE

**There are many more
Daisy picture books to discover:**

- Daisy: Tiger Ways
- Daisy: Eat Your Peas
- Daisy: Really, Really
- Daisy: Yuk!
- Daisy: You Do!
- Super Daisy

BIG TROUBLE

**Join Daisy on these
adventures for older readers:**

- Daisy and the Trouble with Giants
- Daisy and the Trouble with Kittens
- Daisy and the Trouble with Life
- Daisy and the Trouble with Zoos

. . . AND MANY MORE!